'Gum has a shape of i
But when it comes ou
– Hannah Wilke

'Yes, I find myself the best example of evil.'
– Marlene Dumas

Oliver Reed by Hannah Regel

Sorry Gets Hooved

In the opening credits for the 1939 film *The Women* each woman is depicted as an animal to set the tone. Marjorie Main (housekeeper at a Reno ranch for high class women who've failed in love) appears as a yawning horse.

The feet of adult women make impressions in corridors

Little girls want shoes that go clack

A child does not relate the image of it,
hooves, as the echo of shame
we bask in their wrong future

We boil things with hooves,
we sit on them and ride them and make them glue,
we put them inside tracks, shoot saliva at their cash
    hearts

I join in anyway with my oblivious desire,
banging two coconuts

> (Wild light watched from all sides
> allowing the subject to become a stain
> surveyed everywhere, with age
> her carrier bag skin elucidates
> dandelions softening in the weft)

The girls are paid to babysit for a woman they have
  just met
in a car park. They tell the girl they are sitting to say Ass
She says No, they say Do It

The little girl says Ass and then she says Bitch

The girls give the girl they are sitting a makeover
They smear makeup all over her face it looks bad
They are sort of laughing at her while they do it

After this they are bored
They decide to play hide and seek
The little girl's mother comes back
asks where her daughter is
The girls say they don't know. It is very dark
when this happens and they are in the woods

I pick the sole off my shoe
to omit one more person
from being a teenage girl
do not look like that, I know
such an ancient and cruel thing
cannot ever be erased
but the fanciest dream of
solitude breaks a lively blood
posing at the headlights
and the swollen hip of poetry
when I am squeezing your knee
when I am being a sucker
when I am wah wah wah
saying softly can you please
warden of your pony mind
and skinny wrists
let me in. Let me show you
the hungers of tiny insects
who live meanly like you do
not knowing about pretty
just crisis and sensation
like you are going to die
every time you bleed
getting spit on your heart
while your sad dad fumbles
and I will myself barren

How do you feel?
I feel angry.
What do you want?
I want to brush my hair

We have laminated for you
everything possible
please point to what you need

Meg Ryan sings to the radio whilst driving along the motorway (before changing the channel to find what is perhaps not a wrong love but certainly an improbable one, existing for at least an hour solely as speculation with her co-worker and wholly based on emulating a film she has seen but is not in). She sings: horses, horses, horses, horses.

No one being able to recognise a door
we crack our noses and discard the shell
the night blows a dust into
writing our middle-years backward

Waking up to the silence of shoulders, perfect lips
and my stomach kissing your back all big and full of

Can you do 7 days, 2 doubles?

I mean, I'd rather do nothing ever
just exist as scattered images already applauded, but
    sure
when can I start? I'll need the money for raising horses
and building catapults for more permanent acts

Define permanence, define catapult
pay all my bills, compost, what else

Being gorgeously useless and full of it
she said: I am the most important artist of my generation
then later, amended: Female artist

(Obedience
reserves light
into the skin
or shaved spots
of cradling pain
plucked eyebrows
visible hips
and hi hi hi
her mother
a martyr
sits alone
on a garden chair

everyone's
an actress
at 2 p.m.)

In the puddles she's ageless
like a tambourine.
Popped posture knowing
how to get to you
death, should she need to,
when final means only
an intermission in the meal-time.
Lacquered ass on the cold floor
of the farmhouse, beheaded
teetering hooved and cold-legged,
for a thumb and a forefinger,
for a fizz squeezed in
to the lime shortened
crotched up
lives of other people
and their giggling plastic cups
all flop and no finesse
in the gap-toothed day
where she tells us,
through her hair:

Art is only good
when you could
at any point
become it

Jane Fonda (who, being loved by no one, can only love wrongly) gets shot in the head like a lame horse after dragging her already dead dance partner over a disco marathon finish line.

Why such an object might elicit both a kick
and a kiss and why nothing might be done
about it are at issue: the fuzzed speech
of vanity as the godhead of revenge

> in sedate male surface
> I train my heart to want
> a mirror above all things
> to see myself
> as an object
> with the charge
> of art
> I soften
> when I think
> about the future
> when I think
> about the future
> I have to get so drunk
> that I make myself stupid
> I have to be stupid
> really stupid
> so that your contempt
> can be educated. Look
> all I'm trying to do is fuck
> up a fantasy so that you
> can walk around
> and feel otherwise

All the furniture is white.
Used tampon trodden on
lipstick spoilt carpet,
multipack of Perrier.
She can't hold her head normal,
has to tilt it back because
her brain fluid won't stay in.
Mum paid for it in the bay
of a straitjacket, she said,
I think about maggots
— their whatever lives

My nose is cute like a button,
just right. We put on Taylor Swift
and she says *that is exactly me*

She was wearing a big fashionable white shirt with a
　　window for her bra in the back
Spilt wine all over it and was talking loudly and I
　　wanted to be her
I want to be the person that spills wine all over their
　　shirt
and still says things to the party like I am the most
　　important artist
to do what I want which is real
Elizabeth Taylor's posture
now that is a big fuck you question mark
Her curling shoulders, they just mean it
like whiskey. Steal a mink
write No Sale on the big mirror
I wish:

Yes

it was me that stuck the finger in
but how dare he with the grit fist of his rightness
make a hole in our boat
the calloused hand of honesty
cringes in the life raft
getting salt in the pact

She goes back to him, Liz
and besides I love him
I wash my feet in the leaks eating sorry toffee

I would never punch a hole in a wall because there is
    no evil inside me
I lie
I would never punch a hole in a wall because I am too
    vain
to move my body in ways that make it animal. This is
    a kind of evil
because I am an animal. I am. See? Just yesterday I
    dropped a fish finger on the floor
Because no one was there to see it fall I put it on his
    plate, not mine. My evil
it sits in its avoidance, in making other people dirty
there is a kind of pleasure

Tippi Hedren, in Hitchcock's *Marnie*, tells Forio (the horse), "If you wanna bite somebody, bite me."

When no one is home I stand unclothed and mimic the
    movements of swans on YouTube
The dry heave of this fulfilment fills the soft room of time

The weather is getting warmer and my eyes are rising up

I want my life to change. I want my life to change but
    I am not brave
and I speak from the throat not the belly like I should
want to shed my womanhood
blowing cigarette ash from the cuff of a coat
so flimsy and unwanted, but I have put the dream of
    being small
and cherished in my optimistic heart, repeating forever
under his big hard borrowedness. There is no changed
    water here
just other people, you have to pick them
and we do, but I could not tell you how or for whom
we repeat what we endure, so blissful is this
life that we drink from and never spill out
from. Lapping like a bird
my own enemy, doing exactly as I'm meant

And there was never a sin so boiled
as the reluctance to be what is not yet told

to the herd

Unmask yourself!

I've paid my two cents
I want to see what I've got

Well, Sir, for a start
I've given up on being interesting
And a good life, what does that take?
Sharp elbows. That's what!
I've seen the film I know how it goes
All the cards on the table
show a woman alone
on a tall hill
                    Sure,
I never said I want to be alone
I said I want to be left alone
There is all the difference
How straightforwardly
a woman
disrobes
I stand in that nakedness
feeling for a face,
my own trembling,
the taunting from beneath
whilst the problem
holds itself wanting

Marilyn Monroe (upon learning that the horses caught by her lover Clark Gable will be sold for dog food) walks out into the open expanse of a salt flat and screams.

My brain being woollen and so
this small glass, a lace for
the day, a writing bribe,
has it beat you out of words?
Or got you drunk? Frantic
under ground lids. Four lemons
and a pair low tide, unknown
purple hands—I've stared into
the promise well for eight years now,
asked for money politely
each day. Art here is a joke,
an eating contest: embodied
responses to faking it. I
take out a hair pin
and get to work against
that wooden scene. Everyone I know
has one finger in the revolution
and the other in their own eye
—singing
I'm an optimist, honest,
I ate my twin in the womb

Sorry is a Girl, Grown Up

Smack

I took the day in the eye
and clawed it into four walls
in the hours that fail at boredom
but body forth a net

Your bite featured
a birth place
clicking through to greet the floor

Smacking it out that grease panel
working up to bloom a threat
my hunger knuckle danced
star-fuckery, blood-heavy

Heaven,   in your full-fat skull

June

Too long indoors
perhaps is better
than I know it
better than it
                    be
push the cold beer
on moving backs
it takes three trains
to watch the women
fight it makes me feel
alive watching them
I want a smack
fair, organised
running into
tight ab vodka shots
big chandelier
the toilets stink
like a welding bay
it's real here
we are so pumped
to see it clear
slap the banister
smell the smell the
uncooked ferity
the impulse to
throw yourself at
moving trains
slinging it back
fortune/loud
it would be so
easy to make
the jump

squatting on the
big stage, citrus under
nail, getting thin
raking it in
                baby
I cannot protect
you from anyone
else I will brush
your hair only once

Oliver Reed

There is a picture of you
behind the bar where we eat French
sausage and are drunk and I think I know
since a child, your huge hairy face,
that I love you very purely. Always have.
You smoulder a mobile furnace —
one never thinks, on the screen,
that there on the other side
is an embryo, a living lusting
flesh, being put out of play
because you've got a mask on,
                    Oliver Reed
Face of the Old Game, birthed
in the crochet of rape
                    I lift a little finger
and taste the Merguez juice from my chin

The Simple Life

He said get over here, but first he grunted
a little erotic prickle, that grunt: like a penis
twitching in sleep, to get
he said, where's your face,
then put himself inside it. As a child
that was how everything reached my mouth,
from a love to please and impress:
black olives, salted anchovies, even snails once.
Isn't she curious? And now
here you are!

Eviction Notice

A woman is for querying, pursuit and servitude,
    cosmetic scorn
remorselessly it is imagined
we come to some conclusions here where the manacled
    heart breaks

Above stray curls, battered flies and stained lips
like money begets money
and inexpressivity: allowances for card carrying
    blondes: a house!

Worthy sources distinguished through insecure
    environments
which is no new news against depth; those who, in the
    race for acclaim, occasionally
dent the peace-loving sense of how I loathe to lose
    myself in the fullness of creation

Sorry is a Girl, Grown Up

Through domesticity and narrative
we learn about spoilage
I learn that it is a blot
on the day-world, an event
curdled humours. I sorry and spaghetti
falls out of my mouth onto the hob

Instead of a wet sponge I use my face
to wipe it up, because I love
this being my drive, having
cheeks full of don't be cross
the dinner didn't work out

I put my pleasing under the harness
of unhearing and hold tight
scoop those better now cheeks into
a bowl for you, you eat them
For my own good

You just go on my
nerves and
get out of here. Alone
with the morning
pieces of yourself

I walk slowly from that
scene head aching
and sucking a miniature
spoon

Slowly—slowly. Nothing happens
here but the walls
I daydream reasonably
on as he holds my head
like it is his own helmet

Everyone loves a sob story. Eventually
we became addicted to sobbing
its easy rush. Instead of asking anyone
what the sobbing could change

I slip into that sink of dieting time
I have no answers
or barely know anything
Not the colour of my eyes only
their elective wink of silence

I buy a skirt because I am uncertain
about my position in the world
the skirt changes nothing and I return it
arguing small difference into ash
I am too expensive for my life, psychic life
moving coolly from room to room
in what is always
someone else's house

Rendered null, he
plays for broke down glass lines
light hygiene and reserved love
the shoe of air travel and what it allows:
I am far away and only few

A gallant waste of cash

Has anyone congratulated me today? My father
asked if I was Still Making Art
no I am not. The dream I have not proven
has effaced being faithful

Everyone is ugly, once in while
I tempt writing out of spite

In writing I come toward you like a dog
blown over the cellular thump of experience
smoking like a tart baby
subtracting consequence from the anyways
of our already small days

Tight and polished like a conker
your pride sits, seeded within

All straight girls sin for this
some grand fallopian tragedy

Some little laughs...
well, they are gone and I have to stay here

Spanked by the philosopher, a stupid maid
pushing cold hollandaise around a plate

Stuffing tissues into the open mouth of a wage
enough, enough

Inside the roost of a sentence
having nothing to do with this Wednesday

tip-toeing on my skinny escape
of deliberate degradation, where

that plank you offer
walks a bank account

and I beg for it
like baby bio

These little costumed lines are incisions
against the urge. I am addicted to quitting

rats, and pushing my fists into my eyes
committing feeling to a touch that fosters

moving the bluer better chaos to top
you-less, in the infinite living job

taking praise the way a baby takes it
with knuckles in my mouth

Since everyone I know is so intelligent
it seems reasonable that I should get to quit
watch everyone else do a fine job

and besides, I never knew what work was
or what it warranted. I just moved that blue chaos
  around

ran housebound fingers over my bad skin
lodged a five pound note between my two front teeth
no more problems now my job is devoid of language

the only place the poor can go without
any training is show biz. I mean, you just show up

sit on your high stool
pore-less
like a real doll

The matron cries in the doorframe
as we whip the hot boys for the camera

and the lens of painted hatred swivels
in your request for generosity

you have forgotten about those
who cannot fuck without comment

I have never been to Hollywood
but I know it to be true

the furnished dream of a hip bone
softly concave under pale jeans

We muddy the matron's mask
her distress being a Christmas cracker

whoever engages with the tension gets
a miniature Rubik's cube, a red crown

the paper joke of a court jester, asking
hide the knives

too much love for a position
will turn it into the floor then into your face

a bark into explicit legibility
everything being neither real nor forbidden

in the theatre of learnt hysteria
or the trophies your knees can get

Sorry Attends Her Birth

It was shame that hoofed her first
and her heavy glass face
crawling head fore into the carpet
scattering night, small fires, etcetera

The pattern of a human stain in November

Across the floor sat round cartoons of pride; a bunny
joy-strewn with legs drawn out
like a dish

Reclining nude without a drink
aside from the one that hangs permanent inside the
    head
making her jaw so obtuse

Jennifer Lopez, watched by a little boy full of foreboding, coos yeah you like that don't you to a horse stood stationary above red floor markings. A clock ticks loudly in the background running the course of a minute. As the second hand completes a full rotation the horse is very neatly butchered alive along the markings the floor denotes.

What happens is as secret as lip gloss; the earnest
    knots of what is agreed
to be comeuppance in the heavy gallop of young
    mothers

A hem approaching the foot of bird, the stain of a
    threat suckered through the gauze
of maternal advice; some predictions they just spur
    themselves, like

If she carries on like this

Ladders in nylon and a swig, swing, fur hood, frayed
    denim, a park
little bottles of vodka going clink clink click against
    belt buckles, bark chip under nail

Donna Wardman said she didn't think I'd live
end up in a ditch she said, if she carries on like this

How dumb you are though, Donna, how obedient to
    the grill!
all that crawling blowing sucking shined me up real
    good for living

Glistening, dark and smooth like a church step
gently entered forever, I am the polished mouth of
    God

Sarah Jessica Parker (standing outside on the street whist Chris Noth, inside, declares his love for the predictability of some women over others, by choosing the prettier, neater bride) touches the face of a horse; there is recognition.

We beat the earth into the feet of an apology
by this, the skin was hardened artificially
encased: spangled whim, star-face, milk, un-aged

We made it kneel on the floor, it had to drag itself
    around like that
the knees became the hard base of its body. Discuss
    pronouns
because of the kneeling and its implications we had to

She. Gross how it squats in the blood
like a toad we change the locks
there is a lot of guilt about what we made sorry
    become

We lost our bearings in her shame
or our error became her
there are ghosts of the sorry violence everywhere

We can no longer make love
for example: I open my eyes
when you are kissing me and you look full of trust,
    like the word

            sorry

Mike Darnell, head of reality programming at Fox, plugged his show *The Simple Life* to a boardroom full of men with the logic that all people want to see is stilettos in horse shit.

.

Loaded
I do so crawl
that crawl, that crawls
the world over. I do not wet
the foothold right
man man men
howler
extoller
I shall take that
what washes
what evil
my I did
what I can
get
what witnessed
soft thoughts
or night night
night!
Your breast, my root
mixed
straining, behaving
depriving, unbuttoning
gathering, infinite
not
picking, choosing
a head limbs eyes

Mascara wands full of sugar. Fat ambition. Wet knees. Waterloggedschooltrousers. Grazesfilledwithglittering vinegar on soft hands in bowling greens against trees that crawl against hot breath against midriffs against heart against. Eat nothing eat everything that crawls with two fingers down my throat with high waisted belly ring scrunchie roll Charlie Red little bottles of vodka going clink clink click has sick sick sick in your breast my root soft thoughts crawling night gathering bunny grazed soft knees or a head limbs eyes everyone's throat down waterlogged school trousers loaded with sugar picking choosing what I can get what witnessed soft thoughts against hot breath against everyone's throat against heart against heart against heart against sick in glitter in vinegar in bowling greens against trees against men the world over in waterlogged school trousers unbuttoning straining behaving a head your breast my root my breast your root my limbs my eyes my two fingers throat your root full of glitter in bunny grazed soft knees that crawl deprives unbuttoning not picking choosing. That crawl that crawls the world over eats nothing eats everything eats heart eats heart eats heart eats man man men gathering infinite mascara wet knees false sugar sick heart I do so I do so I do so wash what evil my I did

Bright and neat like origami
that folded life approaches mine

She is approximately
young
without opposable target
a morsel dream inside a blowout

Careful —

Beauty is Permission Like Animals Have Hearts

In the line of the bright sun and her trusty red baseball hat, the unicorn women rejoin their friends, a waiter carries a tray, topless women cater to the sunset crowd, cocaine inked on his abs with the word "RUSSIA". A recycled clip from a 2011 film plays on a continuous loop, the summer of her 30th birthday goes on forever. Herself, in a red swimsuit. The image of a person, she gets in and out of cars, betrays no trace of a European accent: I think the time arises, I think the time arises when a woman must be put out to work.

To experience what being a woman really is we degrade
    ourselves through work.
To experience what evil really is we degrade ourselves
    through work.
This is the alchemy.
We hoovered up human remains. Stole the houses birds
    live in.
Suffered in the outposts like saints; impervious to law,
    nature and consequence.
Food had no bearing on our bodies.
A Big Mac held in the future of a void.
We had no civic responsibility, only that of destruction:
reinforcing subjugation, refusing cooperation,
    enhancing contempt.
Destruction is a civic responsibility.
It's like I've always said:
if someone ever asks you to do something for them, do
    it really badly so you never have to do it again.
Like being a woman
or proximate to milk.
We spill it, after Sorrow.
Herding the cows, milking the cows, bottling the milk,
    washing the barn, filling up the troughs.

An unsuccessful barbecue.

You know, among young men the ones who turn out to be great talkers are the ones that get fucked the most.

You know, among young women the ones who turn out to be great talkers are the ones that get fucked the most.

Kill the language. Kill it.

Get the shovel. We're making a belt.

The family room is full of dead deer. The family are proud of what they have killed but the girls who've come to stay are not proud for them, they think it's gross, their faces tell us so. They talk about how they do not like the dead deer or the family that has killed the deer as they break the family swimming pool apart with sledgehammers. They are wearing inappropriate footwear as they break the pool. The oldest boy in the family laughs at them. He thinks they are dumb and he tells them so. He spoils their hair extensions when they aren't looking. They shout hey mister I don't care how many protein shakes egg whites you've eaten I'll kill you I've done it before I'll do it again you better believe it. The girls need money. Family friend Randy has a sausage shop. The family decides the girls will spend a day working for Randy and that is how they will pay for petrol. Their outfits are all wrong for making sausage but it charms. They ask for pink aprons and get blood on their shoes and ankles. They slice the belly and the liver whilst talking about foie gras. The girls like that, they say. They spray minced meat on the walls and the floor. There is meat everywhere. It is on their cheeks and on the clock. They get a can of dog food out from the back of the car, pour it into a pig's intestine, tie it up. It is for the oldest boy, it will show him. They sell the sausages they have made by the side of the road. They hand the sausages through car windows with their bare hands and show their breasts to the drivers as they lean. They save the dog food sausage, though, don't sell that. Setting it aside in a plastic bag they say this one's special. They take it home and feed it to the oldest boy. He doesn't know it is dog food and he likes it, he smiles. The girls look directly into the camera, they say don't mess with us. They drive a pink truck to the next town.

Are you afraid?
Oh no, not of outdoor things.
But you have your indoor fears — eh?
Well — yes, sir.
What of?
Couldn't quite say.
The milk turning sour?
No.
Life in general?
Yes, sir.

Beauty is permission like animals have hearts
We forget sometimes that it is true
For pleasure
In the taste of meat
To enjoy reward
To not question where it came from
Reward
For the violence
Of living

And then suddenly there she was, marching towards us, a potty-mouthed yo-yo, overheated and dehydrated, a damn good actress: hotpants, vertiginous rope-heeled wedges, massive sunglasses skinny and mob-handed with her manager miming zipping her mouth shut.

Text threads across my image,
open air,
horseshoed

She has built it, and her fans.

I mean, in the early days no one even glanced at me. You'd see these beautiful girls, the most chic girls in town, who spent a fortune at the beauty parlour and on their clothes and everyone said darling, you're looking wonderful! And then they'd be ignored. The women, not the men. The men would gather in the corner and start telling jokes or talking deals. The only time they talked about the girls was to say whether they scored with them the night before. People would point me out to Darryl and say, what a sensational girl, and he would answer, just another stock player, we've got a hundred of them, stop trying to push these cunts on me, we've got her for $125 a week. And then, about six months later, Darryl was paying me $400,000, and the men—the men were looking at me—because some stamp had been put on me. I was branded, you see.

Well, then I showed them. You bet. There is no sin worse in life than being boring and nothing worse than letting other people tell you what to do. After that I never had to.

Those days it was just people, places and things. Alligators, hunting rifles, mirrors, chandeliers and camouflage nighties. Buckets of chilled rosè, other people getting trashed, injuries related to car crashes, revenge for something resembling a former lover.

In those days I lived every day like a birthday. A friend of mine came back off patrol from the navy and he was staying in Norfolk, or was it Norway? Anyway, a few months ago he telephoned and asked the publican, who was his father, whether or not I could be given a rum and, well, I'm not used to it, and so I got fairly merry and a friend of mine was staying in the Jamaica, no, the Duke of Normandy! And I was trying to see if he was in there so I went to open the window, just like that, and my hand went right through it. And anyway, it turned out to be the staff quarters, not the room that I was looking for. So I'm standing there, bloodied, in what I thought was my swimming costume because I was due to go swimming, but apparently not! The law tell me: 'lingerie'. So, fair and square, I was shoved in the slammer for a couple of nights. Mischief followed me around.

We used to open bowling alleys and kiss usherettes and I had that kind of surly image, you know? I had some advice once, I got a lot of advice. Actually, the only reason I started acting in the fashion that I do is because I was in a car crash with my ex-wife, simply rolled the thing over and squashed it under a lamp post. I appeared the next day with my arm covered in blood and somebody grabbed it and said are you alright Captain Clegg? And I said I'm hurt, or something like that, probably over the top, and Peter came over to me and said Oliver, what you must remember is that when you're hurt you must always make an understatement of it, don't say yes I'm hurt say yes I'm alright and so I've kept like that ever since. He taught me a great deal, like do nothing, do absolutely nothing. And he did nothing, my dear boy. I'll never forget he went to Brown's Hotel because he'd been kicked out of all the others, got some sandwiches and what have you, then realised he'd forgotten where he was working. So he got a police car, and he said to the police car will you please take me to where I am working? They said Mr. Welles we don't know where you're working and he said you must find out. So he had them all at it. Anyway, in the end he got out of the police car, walked round the corner, found the damn place and when he got in the lift, you'll never believe this, got stuck. Six floors up! It's twelve stories, and he got stuck, and we were waiting, and when he eventually came out, three hours late, he said sorry Michael. And that's what it's about, understatement.

Puffy and swollen, full of bracelets and bulimia gossip,
sprayed to an unnatural sienna, a child model
going crazy once protested:

Can I take a lie? —
They root for me and say they want me to work, then pull
the plug.

She goes down to the nightclub at the Hilton, tobacco
in her mouth, a black eye, milking Gator Bite shots,
Xanax bars...and a pack of cigarettes. Wrecks the
whole air-headed hotel. Pours bleach over the pool
table. Destroys the whole place. Walks past the bar,
scantily clad, using the F word, and for no reason pulls
down the bottom part of her shorts and shows her
behind. Right in front of a couple of kids!

Boxing jumbo, nightcrawlers.

Everyone was in such awe of the violence that we all
just stood back in horror, including the police. And she
just walked out, went to the airport. Even conned some
local boys out of several hundred dollars. Nobody ever
laid a hand on her! I admire her greatly.

I'm telling you this as a father.

The subtle domination of a well-told anecdote is the
language of the father.

The violence of the father.

You're intimidated. You see, it's working.

You know, I'm playing a colonel in my next film and that is why I look extraordinary. I combed my hair and I thought to myself: excuse me! I'm playing a colonel and, devastatingly, I had to pencil in my moustache after four days which proves I'm not terribly virile, but nobody pity me: the reason I'm such a great actress is because I don't know how to lie.

When I have my TV show — which I'd never do, but if I did, or if I called myself a leading voice — I'd have the audacity to say I don't support women like you. Women's liberation will never survive, not while I'm in the kitchen. The women's liberation sometimes does some extraordinary sabotage; I mean the fact that I have been smothered in whiskey, and it is whiskey — I can taste it — pays absolutely no cause to the lady. There are going to be a lot of people that will laugh and there will be several who will be quite indignant. I'm not indignant because this is indicative of the bad manners of a lot of chauvinist ladies. But I'll tell you one thing for free: the women in England are quite good. They are good because they're always in the garden: you can't hear them when they shout. I think that most women, I think that most women are very happy. I really think that most women are happy in the garden. Not because they like it, but because it's where they belong, I mean Shakespeare wasn't a bird was he now. I think that basically women are very happy.

Please understand my sense of humour so you don't think I'm crazy. I only took so many selfies because when I'm super-healthy I'm super-fast and I multi-task, I can do anything: a large scale painting in two hours, an audition, a photo shoot and document it all! It's a joke about social media and vanity and if you don't get that well then there's no hope for you. I hope you've understood that now.

Here's the thing: very simple.
It was on that beach that I got hit and I said to myself
I'm going to get that beach. It's going to be my beach.

Masks frolicking in the waves. Inflexible.

I have no emotion, no feeling.

Several teardrops on the left cheek.
A photo of the actress reading her book: an oceanfront
 chaise.
She's probably deeply troubled and therefore great in
 bed.

You don't like my little noise makers?
I raised them to kick, bite and dress under time.
They are about to get their hands real dirty —
an A for oil spill.

No self-destructive tendencies.
Just degrees of playing along.

Her ankle tag malfunctions.
Alone,
she says softly,

Bloom?

(that's her lawyer)

There's a crawfish in my purse!

It is vibrant, clinging
and afraid.

What of?
Couldn't quite say.
The milk turning sour?
No.
Life in general?
Yes, sir.

Two halves of a hairy shell rammed together. When little girls play at going fast and in charge they wear their death, it figures them: a syntax.

Sorry Leaves the Boat

Believing has made a dumb child of me

I walk with my errors

Tight like little arm bands

Along the plank

As my pigtails swing

In the loop of an apology

As I downward

My best impression of a sucked thumb

Hotness is a miserly place to wait for it

I'll show you owning a face

Really own one.

Fire

I don't want to get up in the morning without my life

My life will be crying my face off, as this is true love
I don't think we should be happy to sit in the room of
   life
I want to do something that feels great!

You want some advice? I'll give you some
None of us want to get to thirty
Without knowing how to use a whip

If you've used it enough
I've certainly used it enough

Crack it

Against my commitment to servitude, how I love it
Against my bad education, the one I wear
Like a hat of lard

Crack it and then you will see
If you find the way to

If you find the way, then you too can be a father
But only God can be God. It makes no difference
If the devil has been defeated or if it is your character

   To take hold of the wind
   To turn your back without the aid of your wings
   To take hold of the wind is pornographic

Being gone, we are all in that armpit
making possible the curmudgeon
of this tired salute upon my choices

with my eyes open and my face as still
and silent as sheep bones on a hill, I wait
but I am afraid this too will become a curl

of austerity, toes stuck together in its mouth
eyes shut on the screen, eerie dead end error as
abortions for the climate make a joke out of desire

and then, she speaks in a tone of voice I have
come to regard as familiar yet different
I have come to regard her voice as familiar yet different

and yet, there is one word that always comes to that
  place
she says it again, there are plenty more
love

that's the word —
where this came from
under a disposable plastic cup

we are all made into forever
daughters, remember
I will sacrifice nothing for this world

if it remains dishonest I will fill it with children
who all have demands, they will pour out their pails
  short
legged like the goat, they will make decisions, truly
their own

The smart ones have bent the salt lick into a signpost for the put-upon, open all hours. They rattle its register like dice. Sally is gagging on the dealer's sole. Dumb as a rug we let her root about the back teeth like some unseemly cat.

Someone has to take the hit, honey

                        said smoothing her hair

one knee on the ledge, neck turned around to face her
    voice
                        so if the feeling

came it could

            bent elbows, flat hands, a little force

                    which is a free thing, force

I am old enough now to be my own mother

I travel to hell with her in a shoe

(echoing unendingly)

Clip clop, clip clop, clip clop

Epilogue

In the hell that I hankered for they built this big bonfire and a cathedral that looked like a lavatory and there were lots of people in black hats and flowers and lots of flames and I, hauled right up there with everyone watching, a real star. I had a button which I could press if it got too hot and they shaved my head and they tied me up and I had an escape hatch and a man with a plastic mask on and asbestos when the wind changed and Russell came along to keep throwing petrol on it shouting words of encouragement — Fantastic! — wild eyes fag dangling out his mouth and when I was actually really burning to death he said damn it damn it damn it.

Acknowledgements

Thank you to Tai Shani and the Arts Council England for making this project possible; to Stacy Skolnik, Sam Riviere, Rose Goddard, Cassandra Troyan and Joe Walsh for their support, edits, attention and suggestions; to Max Prediger and Julian Mader for the design; to Montez Press for everything; thank you to Gerard Ortin, Jago Rackham and Ivan Coleman for their help with photography; additional thanks go to the editors of the following publications, in which earlier versions of this writing first appeared: *Form IV, Scaffold, SALT., Queen Mob's Tea House, The Scores, Hotel* and *Emotional Art Mag.*

Notes

'Why such an object would illicit both a kick and a kiss, and why a museum guard would do nothing about it' is from an anecdote in Anna Chave's essay *Minimalism and the Rhetoric of Power* in which she catches two teenage girls kicking Donald Judd's brass floor box. After kicking the box they discover it is reflective, use it to arrange their hair, then kiss their own reflections – leaving two little greasy lip stains. No one in the museum tells them off. Elizabeth Taylor steals a mink, writes 'No Sale' on the big mirror, then goes back to him anyway, in *Butterfield 8*. 'I never said I want to be alone...' is a quote from Greta Garbo. Mike Darnell actually said 'all people want to see is stilettos in cow shit', but for the sake of cohesion I changed the shit we want to see to that of a horse. Various other lines, phrasings and incidents throughout the book are taken from the interview *You Can't Hurt Lindsay Lohan Now* published in *The New York Times*, *The Simple Life* seasons one to five, Paz de la Huerta's Instagram captions, multiple interviews with Oliver Reed, Anne Carson's *The Gender of Sound*, Thomas Hardy's *Tess of the d'Urbervilles*, and the book *My Lunches with Orson: Conversations Between Henry Jaglom and Orson Welles*.

Oliver Reed by Hannah Regel

Editor: Stacy Skolnik
Design: JMMP–Julian Mader, Max Prediger
Print: Pöge Druck, Leipzig
Edition: 500

Montez Press; Unit 29, Penarth Centre;
Penarth Street; SE15 1TR London; United Kingdom
www.montezpress.com

Supported using public funding by

**ARTS COUNCIL
ENGLAND**

ISBN: 978-1-9160634-7-1